W9-CQP-472

KOOKABURRA

Many people think the kookaburra's call sounds like a human laugh. The call warns other birds to stay away from its territory. When it hunts, the kookaburra sits silently, listening and watching for insects, lizards, snakes, young birds, and small mammals, which it catches in its strong bill.

TAWNY FROGMOUTH

The mottled feathers of the tawny frogmouth look like bark. Sitting perfectly still, the frogmouths are well camouflaged from enemies and from their prey. They roost quietly in trees during the day with their heads turned upward. At night they drop to the ground to capture insects and spiders. The tawny frogmouth builds its nest of sticks on a tree branch. The female sits on the eggs during the day, the male during the night.

WALLABY

Australians use the term kangaroo only for the largest members of the species. All other ground-dwelling kangaroos they call wallabies. Wallabies are furry gray or brown animals that hop along on their hind legs. They have long tails used as props for standing and for balance when leaping. Some wallabies are active during the day and others at night. They like to eat grasses and other plants. Wallabies usually have one baby at a time.

FLYING FOX

The flying fox, a placental mammal, is really a large bat. Flying foxes may live up to thirty years, usually in trees, but sometimes in caves. Their large eyes see very well in the dim twilight. Flying foxes feed on fruit, flowers, leaves, nectar, pollen, and sometimes insects. All bats are important because they pollinate many types of plants. Flying fox mothers have one or two babies at a time.

The emu, the second largest bird on earth, is the largest bird in Australia. It weighs up to 120 pounds and stands up to five feet high or more. The emu can run 30 miles per hour, but it cannot fly. It eats seeds, fruits, flowers, tender foliage, insects and other small animals. After the female emu lays her dark green eggs, she leaves the male to tend them and to care for the chicks.

RINGTAIL POSSUM

The ringtail possum lives in trees, where it builds its nest of leaves and finds its favorite foods – leaves and flowers and tree bark. These small marsupials can leap great distances from branch to branch or from tree to tree. The ringtail possum is so named because it can curl its tail into a ring. It can use its tail for grasping and for carrying nest material. Ringtail mothers usually have two babies at a time, and some have more than one litter each year.

PLATYPUS

The platypus lives only in Australia. It is an odd-looking mammal with webbed feet, a big tail like a beaver, and a flat snout like a duck's bill. The platypus makes its nest at the end of a winding tunnel on the bank of a river or lake. There the female lays one to three eggs. After the eggs hatch, the tiny infants live in their mother's pouch until they mature. Adult platypuses eat insect larvae, crayfish, worms, and tadpoles found in the water near their homes.

ECHIDNA

The echidna is a pudgy little animal covered almost entirely with spines. It has a tiny mouth at the end of its snout and a sticky tongue it uses to lick up ants and termites. A new-born echidna is just over half an inch long. It lives in its mother's pouch until its spines begin to grow. The echidna protects itself from enemies by rolling into a ball and hiding in a crevice or by burrowing quickly into soft ground until it almost disappears.

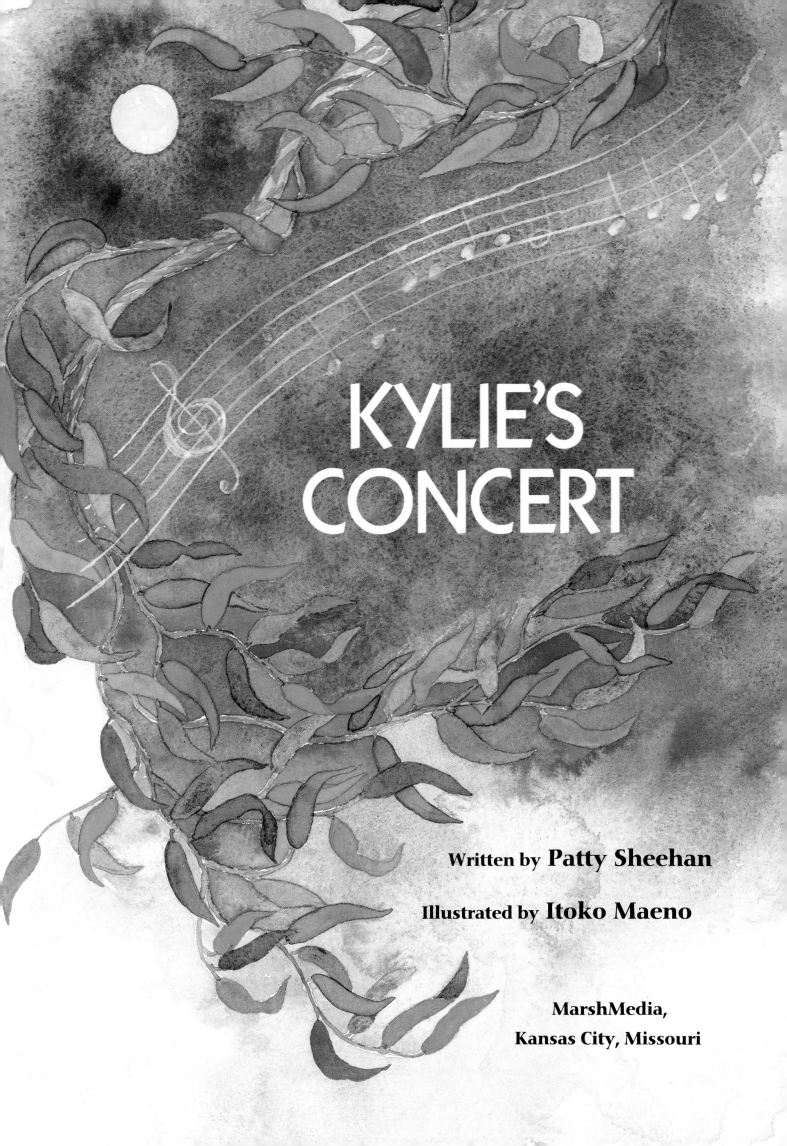

KYLIE'S CONCERT

Written by **Patty Sheehan**

Illustrated by **Itoko Maeno**

MarshMedia,
Kansas City, Missouri

*To all the precious beings who share life
here on our Mother Earth*

Text ©1993 by Patty Sheehan
Illustrations ©1993 by Itoko Maeno

*All rights reserved. No part of this book may be reproduced in any form without
permission in writing from Marsh Film Enterprises, Inc., P. O. Box 8082,
Shawnee Mission, Kansas 66208, USA, except by a newspaper or magazine
reviewer who wishes to quote brief passages in a review.*

Published by **MARSH**media

A Division of Marsh Film Enterprises, Inc.
P. O. Box 8082
Shawnee Mission, KS 66208

Library of Congress Cataloging–in–Publication Data

Sheehan, Patty.
    Kylie's concert/written by Patty Sheehan; illustrated by
Itoko Maeno.
        p.   cm.
    Summary: While exploring the Australian forest and
meeting the different animals who live there, Kylie the singing
koala discovers that they are in danger of being destroyed and
becomes active in saving the forest.
    ISBN 1-55942-046-4
    [1. Koala–Fiction.   2. Zoology–Australia–Fiction.
3. Conservation of natural resources–Fiction.]   I. Maeno, Itoko,
ill.   II. Title.
PZ7.S5395Ky 1993
[Fic]–dc20   92-39683

Special thanks to my parents, Louise and Bill Sheehan;
my brother, Tom Sheehan; Carol Talley; Joan Marsh; the members of
my critique group, Mary Munding, Bruce Williamson, Ken Phillips, Don Jeffries,
Natalie Cunningham, Karlie Rose Harper, Jennifer Burk, Bobbie Brown, Kay Nations;
Larry Burnet; and my many other friends who have encouraged my writing.

Printed in Hong Kong

Book layout by Christine Nolt

One evening not long ago, as the moon lit up the forest path, a dream grew in Kylie's heart. Kylie always sang what was in her heart.

I'll see the forest's treasures
If I follow the path along.
I'll dream the forest's dream
And sing the forest's song.

I'll learn the forest's secrets
If I follow the path along.
I'll dream the forest's dream
And sing the forest's song.

"That's right, Kylie," chirped Willy Wagtail, Kylie's teacher and very best friend. "It's time for you to follow the forest's path. You will dream the forest's dream and sing the forest's song for everyone to hear."

"It will be hard to say goodbye to you and my other friends," Kylie said, "and to my eucalyptus tree."

"Goodbye isn't always forever or always what it seems," said Willy Wagtail. "Trust your heart to guide you."

"Willy's right," Kylie thought as she shinnied down her tree.

She said goodbye to her friends – to Papa Emu and his chicks, to the wallaby and the platypus and the kookaburra, too. With only the moonlight for company, Kylie scuffled off through the bark and seed pods scattered along the forest path.

As Kylie traveled along, the way grew strange and mysterious. Kylie heard something scurry and scratch alongside the path. Out of the corner of her eye, she saw a spiny rock burrow into the dirt.

Startled, Kylie scrambled up the nearest tree. She sat very still and looked down. The spiny rock moved.

A nose poked out of the
dirt. Then a head.

"Who are you?" asked Kylie. "And why
did you bury yourself like that?"

"I'm an echidna. The bowerbird told me a terrible
danger is coming. He was so scared he left his bower.
I thought *you* were the terrible danger, and I was trying
to frighten you away."

"I'm not dangerous," said Kylie.

"Then I don't know what the danger is," the echidna said
as she hurried off. "And I'm not waiting here to find out."

8

Leaves shimmered in the moonlight. Birds sang and bugs hummed. Rustles and calls of other night animals filled the spicy air of the forest.

Kylie looked around. "I'm sure there's no danger here," she said to herself. "And I've seen a forest treasure, the echidna. I even learned a secret. I know how she makes herself look scary."

Kylie sang as she walked along the path:

I love the big and spicy sky
Where the bugs and the birds all fly.

I love the animals upon the ground
With flowers blooming —

Suddenly, something crashed through the branches above her.

It scooted down the tree trunk and landed with a THUMP!

Kylie gasped and bolted up another tree. "Could this be the terrible danger the echidna told me about?" she wondered, peering through the leaves.

A furry creature stood up and brushed himself off. He didn't look dangerous.

"Are you all right?" Kylie called down. "Who are you? Why are you in such a hurry?"

"I'm a tree kangaroo, and I'm all right, thank you. The sugar glider told me a terrible danger is coming. I don't want to be here when it arrives. You'd better not be here either!" With that, the tree kangaroo hopped away.

Kylie looked all around. She listened. She sniffed. "There's no danger here now," she said. "Maybe the danger – if there ever was one – has gone away." She climbed down the tree. "And I saw another treasure, the tree kangaroo. I learned another secret. I know how he scoots down tree trunks when he's in a hurry."

After a while, Kylie came to a stream. Frogs and fish swam between the rocks in clear water.

On and on Kylie walked. Again, she began to sing:

> I love the animals who live in the trees
> In sun and moon and rain and breeze.
>
> I love frogs and fish who swim in the stream
> In the —

Again, Kylie stopped singing. Right by
her ear, a voice warned, "Hurry along!
Hurry along!"

But no one was there.

"Who are you? Where are you?" Kylie called.
"I can't see you."

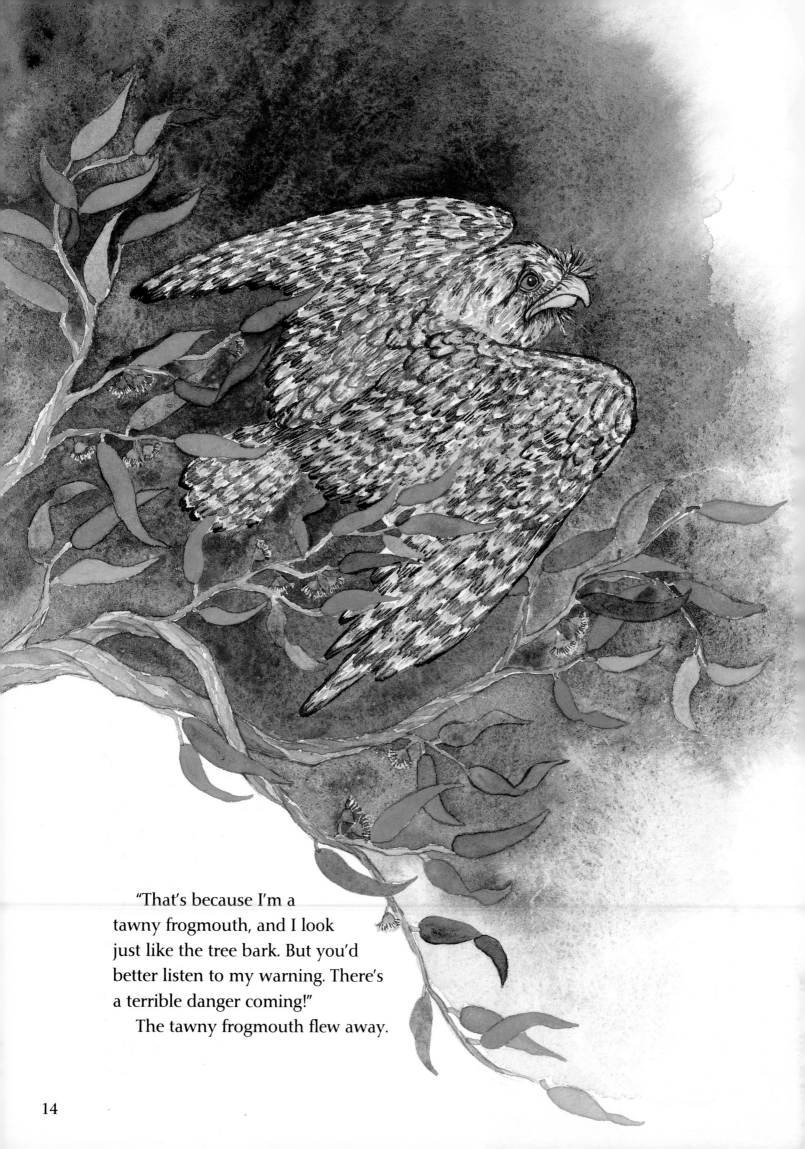

"That's because I'm a
tawny frogmouth, and I look
just like the tree bark. But you'd
better listen to my warning. There's
a terrible danger coming!"
The tawny frogmouth flew away.

14

Kylie shuddered. "Maybe there is a danger," she said as she climbed to the safety of a tall eucalyptus tree. She looked, she listened, and she sniffed. "No," she said, "there is probably no terrible danger coming. And this feels like a safe place to rest." She settled her tired little body into a fork of the tree.

"I saw another treasure, the tawny frogmouth," Kylie whispered. "I learned another secret. I know how he hides in plain sight." And Kylie drifted off to sleep, wishing she could tell Willy about all the things she had seen.

15

Suddenly Kylie woke with a start. She heard a loud RUMBLE RUMBLE RUMBLE and BUZZ BUZZ BUZZ. A flying fox sailed screaming past her. Birds flew wildly into the sky. Animals rushed away across the forest floor.

"What's happening?" Kylie cried.

"The terrible danger!" yelled a ring-tailed possum as he leapt past Kylie into another tree.

A foul smell burned Kylie's nostrils. A bitter taste puckered her mouth. And then Kylie saw it for herself – the terrible danger!

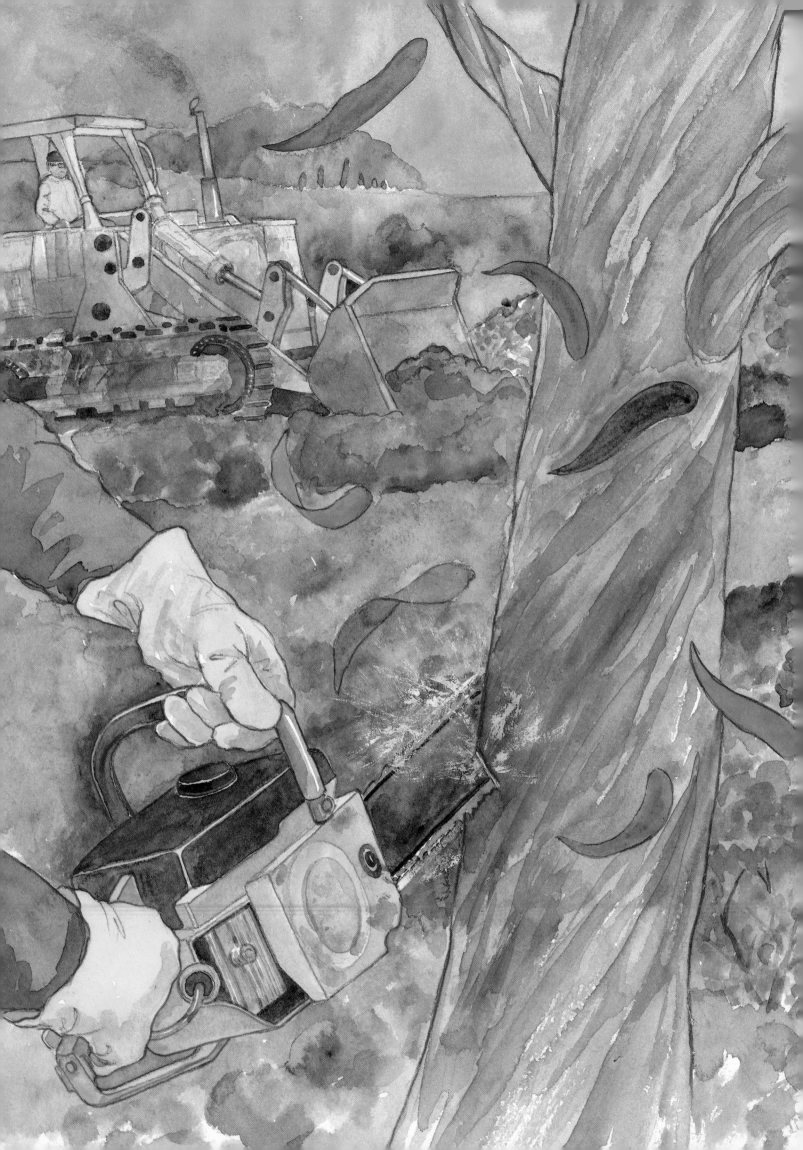

Huge monsters tore at the earth. They ripped up bushes and little trees. They rumbled and shook the whole forest. From the distance, Kylie heard a loud buzzing sound.

RRRRIP! SCREEEEECH! CRACK! A mighty tree crashed to the earth.

"The poor tree!" Kylie cried. "And birds made their nests in the branches. Other animals lived there too!"

All day the monsters tore at the earth and ripped up bushes. All day Kylie hid in the top of the tree and shook with terror.

At last, at the end of the day, the monsters stopped. A sad silence settled over the forest. No birds sang. No bugs hummed. No animals rustled or called.

In the terrible stillness, Kylie thought of all the treasures she had seen and secrets she had learned since she set out on the forest's path.

Then the forest's dream began to grow in her heart, and through her tears Kylie began to sing the forest's song, just as Willy Wagtail had said she would.

I dream of big and spicy sky
Where bugs and birds all fly.

Where animals live upon the ground
With flowers blooming all around.

Where animals live in tall tall trees
In sun and moon and rain and breeze.

Where frogs and fish swim in the stream
In my dream, the forest's dream.

There are treasures I have never seen
In my dream in the forest's dream.

She sang the song again and again. Soon, she heard
other voices from below the tree. Kylie crawled closer
to the ground to see several small creatures looking
up at her. Kylie's ears twitched.

"Don't be afraid, little koala," one said.

"We're here to help you," said
another. Their soft eyes and
gentle voices told Kylie
they were friends.

But just then Kylie saw more strange creatures. Some of them were much larger than the first ones. Two of them carried shiny black things.

Kylie scrambled back up the tree.

"Don't be afraid," one of her new friends called up to Kylie. "They won't hurt you. We are all here to help. We're filming a TV show about taking care of the forest. Please come down. We'll sing your forest song together for everyone to hear."

"Yes, please come down," they all begged.

Kylie didn't understand, but she knew what to do.

She climbed slowly down the tree to a lower branch, and, as she always did, Kylie sang what was in her heart.

> *No one can save the forest alone.*
> *Together we must sing the forest's song.*
>
> *We must dream of big and spicy sky*
> *Where bugs and birds all fly.*
>
> *Where animals live upon the ground*
> *With flowers blooming all around.*
>
> *Where animals live in tall tall trees*
> *In sun and moon and rain and breeze.*
>
> *Where frogs and fish swim in the stream.*
> *This is our dream, the forest's dream.*
>
> *There are treasures we have never seen,*
> *In our dream in the forest's dream.*
>
> *No, no one can save the forest alone.*
> *Together we must sing the forest's song.*

Kylie knew that her song had passed from her heart to the hearts of her new friends – as songs of the heart often do – because they all began singing with her.

The birds sang, too, and the bugs hummed along. Rustles and calls of the forest animals filled the air.

"What a great concert that was!" said one of Kylie's new friends. "And that song will be the theme song of our new television show for the whole world to hear."

Kylie remembered Willy Wagtail's words, "It's time for you to sing the forest's song for everyone to hear."

"Willy was right," she thought happily.

After Kylie's new friends
said goodbye, the moon rose and
lit up the forest path.

Kylie was glad she had followed the path
to this place. She was glad she had dreamed the
forest's dream and sung the forest's song.

Now once again Kylie would trust her heart to guide
her. She shinnied down the tree.

As she walked home, Kylie sang out:

> *Goodbye isn't always forever*
> *Or always what it seems,*
> *When you trust your heart to guide you*
> *And sing out your dreams.*

"That's right, Kylie," a familiar voice chirped from a branch above her.
Kylie knew who it was.

It was her teacher and
very best friend, Willy Wagtail,
who had come to meet her.

AUSTRALIA

Australia is both a continent and a country. It is often called the "Land Down Under" because the entire continent is in the Southern Hemisphere of the world. Australia was settled thousands of years ago by the people known today as Aborigines. In the late 17th century, Europeans discovered the land, and the British settled Australia as a colony in the late 18th century. Because Australia is separated from other land masses, animals that are found nowhere else in the world have developed there.

THE BIRDS OF AUSTRALIA

About 700 species of native birds live in Australia, including the popular kookaburras, the flightless emus and cassowaries, black swans, and more than fifty kinds of parrots.

WILLY WAGTAIL

There are many varieties of these small songbirds throughout the world. They are named wagtails because they flick their tails up and down. Willy wagtails have long, slender bodies, legs, and bills. They feed mainly on insects. Willy Wagtails are well known throughout Australia for singing as they fly through the night.

BOWERBIRD

The male bowerbird builds a bower on the ground and decorates it with colored objects, such as shells, berries, and flowers. He often paints the inside with a mixture of crushed berries, dirt, and saliva. Here the bowerbird performs his courtship dance for the female. The bowers are so intricate that early explorers thought they were built by humans.

THE MAMMALS OF AUSTRALIA

Three kinds of mammals live in Australia: monotremes, marsupials, and placentals. Monotremes lay eggs. When the young hatch, they suckle milk from pores on the mother's belly. The platypus and the echidna are the only monotremes. Marsupials give birth to tiny undeveloped babies, which then develop in pouches on the mother's belly. Australia has about 150 species of marsupials. Placental mammals give birth to babies that have developed inside the mother's body. Most mammals, including human beings, are placental mammals.

SUGAR GLIDER

These marsupials can glide through the air on their wing-like skin flaps, using their fluffy tails to help steer their course. They can leap 150 feet, pulling their bodies upright and landing on all fours. Sugar gliders live in families of seven to twelve animals in the hollows of trees. They feed on eucalyptus nectar, pollen, leaves, and sap, and also on insects.

TREE KANGAROO

Most kangaroos live on the ground, but the tree kangaroo spends most of its time in trees. The tree kangaroo has strong arms and long, curved claws like a bear. It uses its big tail to help keep its balance in trees. The tree kangaroo moves about at night eating leaves and fruit. When startled, it may leap to the forest floor from as high as thirty or forty feet or scoot down the tree trunk like a fire fighter down a pole. Like other marsupials, a tree kangaroo baby develops in its mother's pouch.

KOALA

With its wooly coat, baby face, and plush round ears, the koala looks like a teddy bear, but it is not a bear at all. It is a marsupial. Except for a few in zoos, all koalas live in Australia. A baby koala stays in its mother's pouch for six or seven months, and then it rides on her back until it is a year old. Koalas feed on the leaves and bark of eucalyptus trees. They sleep up to twenty hours a day and are most active at night.